W9-DDP-031

Dear mouse friends,
Welcome to the world of

Geronimo Stilton

THE RODENT'S GAZETTE
EDITORIAL STAFF

Geronimo Stilton
A learned and brainy
mouse; editor of
The Rodent's Gazette

Thea Stilton
Geronimo's sister and
special correspondent at
The Rodent's Gazette

Trap Stilton
An awful joker;
Geronimo's cousin and
owner of the store
Cheap Junk for Less

Benjamin Stilton
A sweet and loving
nine-year-old mouse;
Geronimo's favorite
nephew

Geronimo Stilton

VALLEY OF THE GIANT SKELETONS

Scholastic Inc.

New York   Toronto   London   Auckland   Sydney
Mexico City   New Delhi   Hong Kong   Buenos Aires

ISBN 978-0-545-02132-6

Based on an original idea by Elisabetta Dami.

www.geronimostilton.com

Published by Scholastic Inc., 557 Broadway, New York, NY 10012. SCHOLASTIC and associated logos are trademarks and/or registered trademarks of Scholastic Inc.

Stilton is the name of a famous English cheese. It is a registered trademark of the Stilton Cheese Makers' Association. For more information, go to www.stiltoncheese.com

Text by Geronimo Stilton
Original title *La valle degli scheletri giganti*
Cover by Giuseppe Ferrario
Illustrations by Claudio Cernuschi and Christian Aliprandi
Graphics by Merenguita Gingermouse and Michela Battaglin

Special thanks to Kathryn Cristaldi
Translated by Lidia Morson Tramontozzi
Interior design by Kay Petronio

36 35 34 33 32 31   16/0

Printed in the U.S.A.   40
First printing, January 2008

MY WORST NIGHTMARE

It was late. **Very late**. The new cat clock in my office let out twelve terrifying **MEOWS**. I cringed. The clock was a present from my obnoxious cousin Trap. He loves to scare me, which is easy. You see, I'm a bit of a scaredy mouse, and . . .

Oops, I almost forgot to introduce myself! My name is Stilton, Geronimo Stilton. I

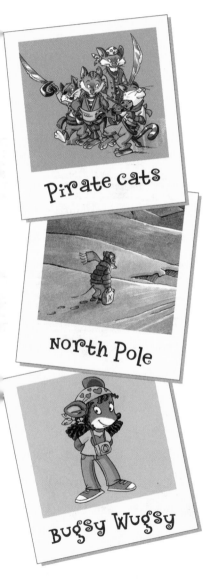

Pirate cats

North Pole

Bugsy Wugsy

run the most popular newspaper in New Mouse City. It's called *The Rodent's Gazette.* I also write adventure books.

In fact, that's why I was still at the office. I was working on my latest novel. Too bad I couldn't think of anything to write.

I stared at the PILE of crumpled papers in my wastebasket. Rats!

My mind was a total BLANK. The only adventures I could think of were ones

I had already written about. Like the time I met a band of PIRATE CATS. Or the time I went to the NORTH POLE. Or the time a pesky little mouse named Bugsy Wugsy and I discovered a **mummy**.

I looked out the window. It was so dark and spooky. Hmm ... that gave me an idea. Maybe I could write a story about GHOSTS!

I shivered as I began to WRITE.

A STORY ABOUT GHOSTS!

CHAPTER 1

It was midnight — the time when all good mice should be home, snug in their beds.

But where was I? I was stuck in a creepy old castle.

That's right. Stuck. Someone or something had locked me inside.

I raced up a long, dark staircase looking for a way out.

At the top of the stairs, I found a small door.

Slowly, I pulled the door open.

Creeaak!

What was behind the door? Who knows! I couldn't type another word. That's because the lights in my office had suddenly gone out.

A voice

pierced the

darkness.

It shrieked,

"GERONIMOOO

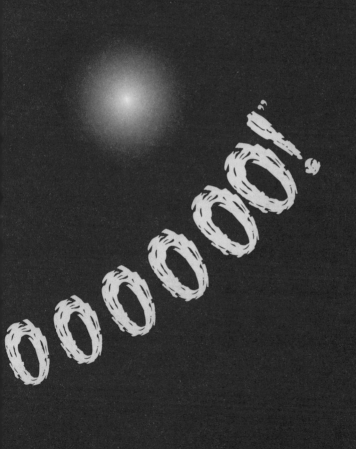

I was scared out of my fur.

"Wh-wh-wh-who is it?" I stammered.

"It is I, your worst NIGHTMARE!" the voice called out. A minute later, the lights

flickered back on. My cousin Trap stood in front of me. He was laughing so hard tears rolled down his whiskers.

"You are such a 'fraidy mouse, Germeister!" he snorted. He plopped down on a chair. He put his dirty PAWS up on my desk. Then he picked his snout.

I GROANED. Oh, why did my cousin have to be so disgusting? He really was my worst nightmare.

"Do you mind getting your paws off my

desk?" I grumbled.

My cousin pretended not to hear me.

Instead he pulled out a large bag of cheese popcorn. Then he began to shovel the popcorn into his mouth like a starving rat. Sticky orange cheese DRIBBLED down his snout. It splattered all over my desk.

I was livid.

"Do you mind?!" I shrieked.

"CAN'T YOU SEE I'M TRYING TO WRITE HERE?"

YOU CAN'T
EVEN WRITE A
SHOPPING LIST!

My cousin rolled his eyes. He pointed to the papers spilling out of my wastebasket.

"Looks like you're not writing much, anyway," he smirked. "What's the matter, Gerry Berry? **Fresh out of ideas**?"

Now I was really **FUMING**. For one thing, I hate it when my cousin calls me Gerry Berry. And another thing, I hate it when he's right. I *was* fresh out of **ideas**. I was even fresh out of stale ideas. My mind was a **TOTAL BLANK**.

But I wasn't about to let Trap know that. With a squeak, I began typing away like a **MANIAC**. I'd show him I wasn't all

WASHED UP. I typed faster and faster. My paws practically flew over the keys.

What was I writing about? My trip to the Costa Rican **RAINFOREST**? My journey across the Ratlantic Ocean? Well, not exactly. To be honest, I wasn't writing an adventure story at all. I was busy typing out a **shopping list**. I hadn't been to the Stop and Squeak in a few days, and there was hardly a nibble left in my refrigerator.

I was so **BUSY** thinking about food that I almost forgot about my cousin. Just then, I realized

SHOPPING LIST:
cheese
milk
sugar
flour

Out of ideas, Gerry Berry?

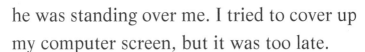

he was standing over me. I tried to cover up my computer screen, but it was too late.

"What's this, Germeister? **Cheese, milk, flour?** You're not writing a new novel. You're writing a *shopping list!*" he squeaked with a smirk.

I sighed. "Okay, I'll admit it," I muttered. "I'm having a little trouble coming up with ideas."

My cousin snickered. He pulled a **MAGNIFYING GLASS** out of his back pocket. He held it up to his eye, then pretended to peer deep in my ear.

Hhmmmmm...

"Anyone home?" he squeaked. "You're right, Gerrykins. It looks like your brain has completely skipped town!" He laughed so hard a button popped off his shirt.

I **gROaned**.

But before I could run out the door, Trap threw his paw around my shoulder.

"Don't worry about the old brain, Geronimoid. I've got just the **CURE**. You see, I've brought you a little present. A present that will leave you **bursting** with ideas," he said.

That's when I noticed Trap had placed something on my desk.

It was a very, very old-looking piece of *yellowed paper*. The paper was wrapped around a gigantic bone.

How strange! A gigantic bone . . .

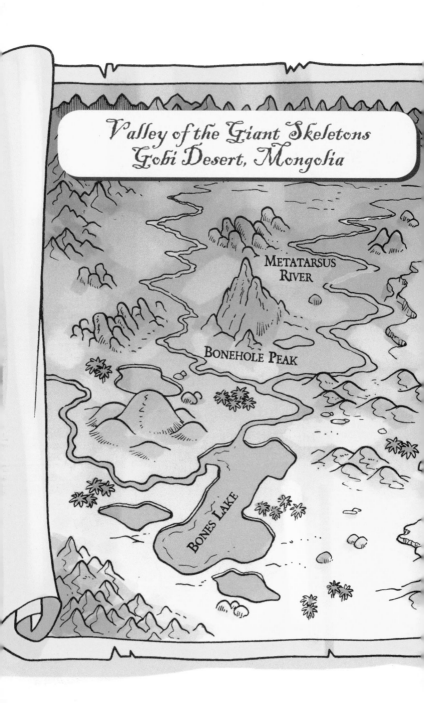

MYSTERY MOUNTAINS

VERTEBRAE GROTTO

TIBIA HILLS

PLAINS
OF SECRETS

THE TREASURE LIES HERE!

A Map of Mongolia

"Check this out, Germeister," my cousin squeaked. Carefully, he slid the document off the bone. I was so intrigued I didn't even mind the name-calling.

The yellowed paper was actually an old map. I picked up the **MAGNIFYING GLASS** and peered at it closely.

It was an old map of the Gobi Desert in Mongolia. But there were odd names written on it.

Valley of the Giant Skeletons

Bonehole Peak

MYSTERY MOUNTAINS

Metatarsus River

Vertebrae Grotto

BONES LAKE

Plains of Secrets

Tibia Hills

I squinted at my cousin.

"How do you know this map is **REAL**?" I asked, my mind filling with doubt.

Trap's eyes sparkled. "I know it's *real* because I found it!" he squeaked proudly. Then he lowered his voice mysteriously.

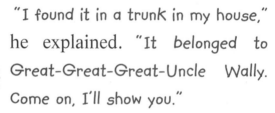

"I found it in a trunk in my house," he explained. "It belonged to Great-Great-Great-Uncle Wally. Come on, I'll show you."

We left the office and headed for Trap's house.

Do you know where my cousin lives? It is a very unique place. You see, he lives in an old train car called the *Orient Express*. It belonged to our Great-Great-Great-Uncle Wally, also known as Wandering Wally. He lived in the 1800s and was an explorer. He was always roaming around the world

Wandering Wally's Chest

in search of mysterious treasures.

Uncle Wally had turned the train car into a beautiful home. It has a comfortable living room, cozy dining area, and even a small breakfast bar. And of course, there is plenty of LIGHT in the train because of all the windows!

In the sleeping compartment, there's an antique bed with a beautiful BRASS headboard. And for guests, there's a small bunk bed that goes up or down with the pull of a lever. The bathroom is made of the finest MARBLE, and the faucet is solid GOLD.

ORIENT EXPRESS

The Orient Express first began operating in 1883. It was the first European train with sleeping cars and a restaurant car. Its luxurious coaches carried the most famous people. Even today, one can ride in this legendary train, retracing the classic route from Venice, Italy, to Istanbul, Turkey!

TRAP'S

1. BATHROOM
2. TRAP'S BED
3. BUNK BED FOR GUESTS
4. KITCHEN

HOUSE

5 TABLE

6 VELVET SOFAS

7 BREAKFAST BAR

8 COFFEE MAKER

Uncle Wally Stilton's Trunk

When we got to his house, Trap led me straight to the bedroom. I tried not to notice the piles of dirty laundry, cobwebs, and three half-eaten cheese sandwiches on the floor. Did I mention my cousin is a **total slob**?

"This is where I found it," Trap squeaked, picking up one of the old sandwiches and shoveling it into his mouth. "About a month ago, I dropped a coin next to my bed. When I bent down to pick it up, I noticed there was a **hidden button** on the wooden platform. I pushed it and suddenly a secret compartment popped out. Inside it was this trunk!"

Trap showed me a big WOODEN

AT THE BASE OF THE BED, THERE WAS A SECRET BUTTON. I PUSHED IT . . .

. . . SUDDENLY, A SECRET COMPARTMENT POPPED OUT . . .

. . . INSIDE IT WAS THIS TRUNK!

TRUNK. It was locked with a large padlock. Stamped on the lock were the initials **W.S.**

Trap fit a tiny key into the lock. Then he opened the trunk.

I let out an excited squeak. The trunk was filled with all the different things Uncle Wally had used on his *ADVENTURES*. There was an old pick, a lamp, and a flat dish for

Gold Rush

PICK TO DIG IN THE MINE

OIL LAMP

PAN TO SIFT FOR GOLD IN THE RIVER

Mousehara Desert

CANTEEN

EXPLORER'S HAT

COMPASS

Gulf of Mexico

SPYGLASS

panning gold. There was a compass he had used when he searched for treasures in the **GULF OF MEXICO**. There was even a canteen he had carried when he crossed the **Mousehara Desert**.

There was a paddle he had used on the **Amazon River**. There was an old pair of skis he used when he went to the **North Pole**, too — and much, much more!

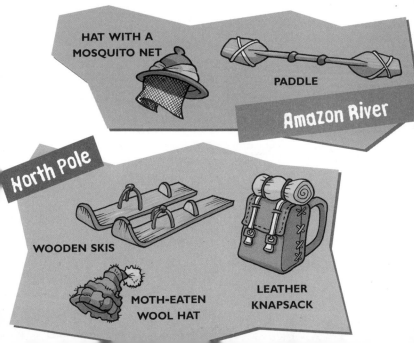

HAT WITH A MOSQUITO NET

PADDLE

Amazon River

North Pole

WOODEN SKIS

MOTH-EATEN WOOL HAT

LEATHER KNAPSACK

CHEWED TO BITS!

Trap reached deep into the trunk and pulled out a leather-bound book.

"This is Uncle Wally's diary," he said. "You won't believe all of the **COOL STUFF** he did. Cheese niblets, was he daring! He kind of reminds me of myself — **STRONG**, *fearless, incredibly handsome*. . . ."

Did I tell you my cousin is terribly conceited?

"Too bad Uncle Wally had to lose his whiskers in such an awful way," he went on.

I was **INTRIGUED**. "What do you mean?" I asked.

My cousin gnashed his teeth. "Didn't you know, Gerry Berry? Old Wally got his fur chewed to bits by a crocodile in the **Amazon River**!" he squeaked.

I began my trip in search of treasures in the Valley of the Giant Skeletons in Mongolia.... That's where I'll be soon, if I don't first get eaten by a crocodile here in Amazonia. Ha, ha, ha, ha, ha!

WALLY STILTON

I gulped. I was still thinking about Uncle Wally and the croc when Trap waved the map in front of my snout.

He pointed to a big ✖ at the bottom of the map. "You see this spot, Gerry Berry? This is where a **TREASURE** is hidden. And we're going to find it. Yep, you, Thea, Benjamin, and I are going to the **Gobi Desert** in Mongolia. When we find this treasure I'll be **RICH, RICH, RICH**!"

I scratched my fur. "But how do you know there's really a treasure hidden there . . . in **MONGOLIA**?" I asked.

Trap smacked me on the head with the map.

"Of course there's a **TREASURE** there! It's right here in the diary. It's what Uncle Wally was searching for before he got **CRUNCHED** into smithereens," he insisted.

I cringed. I wished my cousin would stop talking about the croc chewing up Uncle Wally. It was making me **QUEASY**. But I wasn't about to mention it. My cousin already thought I was a wimp.

"Well, all right. I'll come with you," I said. "But I'm not doing it for the **TREASURE**. I don't care about **MONEY**. I'd just like to bring a happy **ending** to Uncle Wally's last **misadventure**."

Trap chuckled.

"Oh, Germeister, you're such a sap," he said with a smirk.

I WANT YOUR MONEY

A few minutes later, Trap called Thea and Benjamin. It didn't take long to **convince** them to join us on the trip.

My sister Thea loves traveling anywhere and everywhere. She is a real **adventure** mouse. She can climb the steepest mountain in no time flat! She never even gets out of breath. She loves bungee jumping, parasailing, scuba diving, and whitewater rafting.

I guess you could say she's the total opposite of me. I get **exhausted** when I walk and chew gum at the same time!

As for my nephew Benjamin,

Hello?

Hello?

he's the sweetest little mouse you'll ever meet. He's smart and polite and always in a good mood. He loves to go on ADVENTURES, especially when yours truly comes along. Yes, I'm proud to say that I am Benjamin's favorite uncle. See, I told you he was smart!

After Trap talked to our FAMILY, he put his paw around my shoulder.

"Did I ever tell you that you're my favorite cousin?" he gushed.

Uh-oh. Now I knew something was up. My cousin is only **NICE** to me when he wants something.

"What do you want to borrow this time, Trap? My golf clubs, my car, my limited edition Cheese-matic cheese grater?" I asked.

My cousin laughed in my face.

"Don't be ridiculous, Geronimoid. I don't want your silly old golf clubs. I want your **MONEY**. TWENTY THOUSAND DOLLARS, to be exact. That should cover our expenses on the trip," he announced.

I squeaked. I squealed. I ran around in circles chasing my tail. But in the end, I agreed to give Trap the money.

What else could I do? We owed it to Uncle Wally to find that treasure.

All right . . .

Thanks!

I'VE GOT MAIL!

That night, I COULDN'T SLEEP a wink. We were leaving on our trip the next morning. I was a bundle of nerves. For one thing, I hate traveling. Plus, I knew next to nothing about Mongolia.

Then I got an idea. I decided to call my friend Petunia Pretty Paws. Do you know Petunia? She's the most *fascinating* mouse.

She's a TV reporter who goes around the **WORLD** reporting on the environment and different ways to protect **nature**. She's also beautiful. You may have guessed I have a huge **CRUSH** on her. Too bad I turn into a stuttering fool when I talk to her!

Two minutes later, I got Petunia on the phone. "Hi, Geronimo, it's Petunia. I mean, hi, Petunia, it's Geronimo," I stammered. Then I **BLUSHED**. See what I mean?

I told Petunia about our trip. "What do you know about **MONGOLIA** and the Gobi Desert?" I asked.

Petunia explained that it was the rainy season in Mongolia. She said we'd get hit with torrential rains. She also

PETUNIA
PRETTY PAWS

34

said that the sun would **FRY** our fur in the desert.

Soaking rains? BURNING SUN? I flew into a panic. I wasn't an adventure mouse! I liked air-conditioning, bubble baths, and my cozy bed at home. Oh, why had I agreed to go on such a horrible trip?

But Petunia insisted that Mongolia was an **amazing** place.

A few minutes later, the computer began humming.

"I've got mail!" I exclaimed.

It was an e-mail from Petunia all about Mongolia. . . .

MONGOLIA

Area: 603,909 square miles

Population: 2,832,224

Neighbors: Russia to the north and China to the south, east, and west

Capital: Ulaanbaatar

Government: Republic

Language: Khalkha Mongol

Money: Tugrik

Climate: Extreme continental climate with temperatures ranging from -57°F to 96°F in the capital city.

It's also called Outer Mongolia to distinguish it from Inner Mongolia, an autonomous region of China.

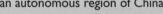

GEOGRAPHY

Known as the "Land of Blue Sky," Mongolia is mostly a high plateau with mountains, salt lakes, and vast grasslands. In the west is the great Altai mountain chain. It is a very rugged region where many nomadic tribes live.

The northern area has large lakes, prairies, and the taiga. The taiga is a biome with thick forests of pine, fir, larch, and sequoia trees.

Plains of short grasses known as "steppes" and the plateau region extend from the center to the eastern part of the country.

In the south, the scenery is dominated by the Gobi Desert, which is also the least populated area.

CLIMATE

Ulaanbaatar is probably the coldest capital city in the world. Temperatures drop below freezing in October, sometimes reaching as low as -22°F in January, and stay below freezing until April. In the Gobi Desert, summer temperatures hit 104°F, but winter winds cause the mercury to plummet to -22°F or even lower. Dust storms kick up in spring, and July and August have frequent downpours.

THE FAUNA

Mongolian traditions and customs are handed down from one generation to the next. A very important part of their culture is deep respect for nature and all living things. For example, Mongolian boots (gutul) have the tips pointing upward so as not to hurt little animals while walking.

According to ancient Mongolian beliefs, there are five sacred animals: the horse, the camel, the yak, the goat, and the sheep.

In Mongolia, there are some very rare

species of animals such as the kangaroo rat, the Gobi bear, the wild camel, the Przewalski's horse, and the snow leopard.

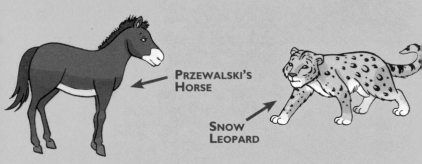

PRZEWALSKI'S HORSE

SNOW LEOPARD

GENGHIS KHAN

Genghis Khan, Mongolian for "Universal Ruler" or "Emperor of All Emperors," became the title of the legendary conqueror Temujin (ca. 1162–1227). The son of a tribal chief in the western part of Mongolia, Temujin was known as an intelligent, brave, and adept fighter.

In 1206, after a series of victories, he was named supreme leader of the Mongol tribes and given the title of "Genghis Khan." Then, he began to extend his rule to other territories and founded the Mongolian Empire, the biggest in history.

Genghis Khan conquered Manchuria, attacked the Great Wall of China, and after a long siege, captured Beijing in 1215. He was also successful in subduing the Turkish-Iranian Empire.

At the time of his death, his empire extended from the Pacific Coast of China to the Caspian Sea, and from the Persian Gulf to Siberia. To this day, Genghis Khan is remembered as a hero by the Mongolian people.

A TRIP TO MONGOLIA

The next morning, I met my family at the airport in New Mouse City. I was a NERVOUS WRECK. I had stuffed three packs of cheese chewing gum, five air-sickness bags, and a relaxation tape in my carry-on. Did I mention I'm **afraid of flying**?

Before boarding the plane, Trap pulled each of us aside. "Remember, don't tell anyone about Uncle Wally's TREASURE," he warned. "It's **top secret**!"

Two minutes later, we were on our way to Ulaanbaatar, the capital of Mongolia. I stared out the window and tried not to think about the fact that we were FLYING. Of course, watching the clouds drift by didn't help. Then I remembered Petunia had suggested I read *A Guide to Mongolia*. I pulled it out and buried my nose in reading. It was fascinating!

The only thing more fascinating was the gorgeous blonde rodent sitting next to me. She was tall and slim and wore tinted BLUE glasses. Everytime I looked her way, she smiled. Too bad I am so shy around pretty mice! Before I knew it, we had landed.

It was SWELTERING HOT in Mongolia, but our journey was far from over.

The next thing I knew, we were climbing aboard another PLANE. This one was much smaller than the first. It looked like it had been through the **Great Cat War**! I wanted to scream. But then I saw the beautiful blonde rodent. **She was getting on the small plane, too**. I buckled my seat belt, and we took off into the sky. What else could I do? I wondered if the blonde rodent had read any of my books.

Before I had time to ask, we landed. I was so happy, I kissed the ground.

A plane . . .

A bus . . .

"What a 'fraidy mouse." Trap smirked. Then he ushered us onto a ratty old **BUS**. I groaned. Oh, how I hate to travel! The bus took us to the edge of the desert. It was a long and bumpy ride. The only good thing: **The blonde rodent sat next to me on the bus.**

When the bus stopped, I practically fell down the steps. I was **hot**. I was **tired**. I was ready for a cold drink and a deep fur massage at my favorite day spa. Unfortunately, Trap had other ideas. He pointed at a **caravan of camels.**

A camel?

"Hop up, Gerrytails," he insisted. The next thing I knew, everyone in my family had mounted a camel. That is, everyone in my family except yours truly.

"I can't do it!" I wailed. What if the camel kicked me? What if I got thrown off its back? I didn't want to die in the desert!

I was just about to give up when I spotted something. It was the blonde rodent. **She was riding a camel up ahead**. A tribe of Mongolian mice led the way.

The next thing I knew, I was clinging to the back of a **CAMEL**. It took off at a gallop.

Help me! I'm scared!

GERONIMO STILTON'S TRIP IN MONGOLIA

ULAANBAATAR

DALAN

DZADGAD

GOBI DESERT

PLANE

SMALL AIRPLANE

BUS

CAMEL

A FASCINATING
BLONDE RODENT

After many hours of riding, the caravan stopped to rest for the night. We ate dinner, then everyone gathered around the FIRE. Lucky for me, I was seated right next to the beautiful blonde rodent. She smiled at me. Her teeth were so WHITE, I practically fell off the rock I was sitting on. I opened my mouth to introduce myself, but suddenly I couldn't REMEMBER my name.

Then she spoke. "Excuse me, but aren't you *Geronimo Stilton*, the publisher of *The Rodent's Gazette*, the most famous newspaper on Mouse Island?" she asked.

KARINA
VON FOSSILSNOUT

I BLUSHED. "Yes, um, the publisher, I am, that is, *Geromino Stilton*," I stammered.

Her smile grew wider. "I'm Karina von Fossilsnout," she said, shaking my paw.

Then I really did fall off my rock. I could hardly believe I was shaking paws with Dr. Karina von Fossilsnout! Do you know Dr. von Fossilsnout? She is very famouse. She is the director of the **MOUSEUM OF NATURAL HISTORY** in New Mouse City. She specializes in paleontology, the study of fossils.

We chatted by the fire long into the night. Karina was the most charming mouse. She told me she loved my books.

"Did anyone ever tell you that you are an incredibly *intelligent*, *handsome*, and *brilliant* mouse?" she asked.

I was on **cloud nine**. Karina asked me a

thousand questions. Then she asked me why I had come to Mongolia.

I knew I shouldn't have spilled our **secret**, but I couldn't help myself. I told Karina all about the **MAP** Trap had found.

"We're going to search for the TREASURE," I explained.

Thea overheard me and shot me a look. I ignored her. Karina was such a sweet mouse. I knew I could trust her with our secret.

That night, I spoke to another sweet mouse. Petunia Pretty Paws called me on my cell phone.

I told her that I had met Karina. Petunia was shocked.

"That's so strange," she squeaked. "Dr. von Fossilsnout told me she **hates** to travel. She hardly ever leaves the mouseum."

MY NAME IS BONDI BOBIRAT

The next morning, I looked for Karina, but she had **mysteriously** vanished. The head of the caravan told me that she had left at dawn. I was surprised and disappointed.

I had been looking forward to spending the day riding and chatting with Karina. Instead, I would just be riding. Yep, riding

BONDI BOBIRAT

my crazed camel. Yesterday, I had bet my fur it was trying to throw me off its back.

Now it shot me an EVIL LOOK. I shivered. But before I could climb onto the camel's back, a short, skinny rat with curly whiskers approached me.

"Oh, you poor rodent. You look exhausted! How would you like to travel by car instead of **smelly** camel?" He grinned. "My name is **BONDI BOBIRAT**, and I would be happy to be your **GUIDE** and drive you wherever you are headed."

I could hardly believe my good luck. Bondi Bobirat had a **SHINY** new Jeep. And his **RATE** was dirt-cheap.

I was all ready to go when Benjamin tugged on my sleeve. "Be careful, Uncle Geronimo," he whispered. "Something seems funny about that rat."

I patted Benjamin on the head. "Don't be silly, Nephew! He is just trying to help us. You'll see," I assured him.

I told Bobirat we were headed for the **Valley of the Giant Skeletons**. Then I

showed him Uncle Wally's **map**. But before Bobirat had a chance to read it, Trap ripped the map out of his paws.

"I don't trust that rat," my cousin WHISPERED to me.

I *coughed*. Oh, why did my family have to be so embarrassing?

Luckily, Bobirat didn't seem to notice. "Climb on in," he said to Trap warmly. "I've got lots of food for you to munch on."

At the mention of food, my cousin's eyes lit up. He began to drool like a starving mouse at an All-You-Can-Eat Cheddar Bar.

"Well, what are we WAITING for, Geronimoid? LET'S GO!" he declared. Then he HOPPED into the Jeep.

The rest of the family followed, and we roared off into the desert.

We traveled all day. And the next day. And the day after that.

I was beginning to worry.

Why weren't we there yet?

ARE WE THERE YET?

By the third night, I was in a **panic**.

"We told you not to trust that rat," my family complained.

I took **BONDI BOBIRAT** aside.

"How long until we reach the **Valley of the Giant Skeletons**?" I asked him.

He shrugged his shoulders. Not a good sign.

"Do you even know where the valley is?" I pressed.

Again, he shrugged his shoulders. Not good at all.

By now, I was beginning to get a mouse-sized **HEADACHE**.

My family was right. I should never have trusted Bondi Bobirat. He probably couldn't find his way out of a bag of cheese chips!

But before I could tell him so, Bobirat held up his paw. "I know you're not happy, Mr. Geronimo," he squeaked. "But we could get where we're going a lot *FASTER* if I could just sneak a peek at your map."

With a **sigh**, I took the map and handed it to Bobirat. What else could I do? We couldn't drive around the desert forever.

As soon as he saw it, Bobirat's eyes LIT UP like the Christmas tree at Ratville Center.

IT'S ALL YOUR FAULT, GERONIMO STILTON!

That night, I lay in my sleeping bag staring up at the stars. What a beautiful sight. I wished **Dr. von Fossilsnout** had stuck around to see it.

It was so strange how she had left without saying good-bye. Oh, well. Maybe there was an *emergency* back at the mouseum.

The next morning, I woke up bright and early. We were finally going to reach the Valley of the Giant Skeletons! Then I noticed something that made my fur stand on end. There were **THREE THINGS** missing from the campsite.

BONDI BOBIRAT   **THE MAP**   **THE JEEP!**

Moldy mozzarella balls! Now I had to face **THREE PROBLEMS**:

My family threw a fit.

"We told you not to trust that rat!" they squeaked at the top of their lungs. Well, all except Benjamin. He just looked disappointed.

I chewed my whiskers. "Don't worry, I know we're in the middle of the *desert*, it's SWELTERING HOT, and we have no car, no food, no water . . ."

Before I could stop myself, I was sobbing uncontrollably.

Thea marched over.

"Stop your whimpering right this second! Let's go!" she ordered.

Did I mention my sister is the exact opposite of me? Yep, she's one take-charge kind of mouse.

MY COUSIN TRAP

MY SISTER THEA

MY NEPHEW BENJAMIN

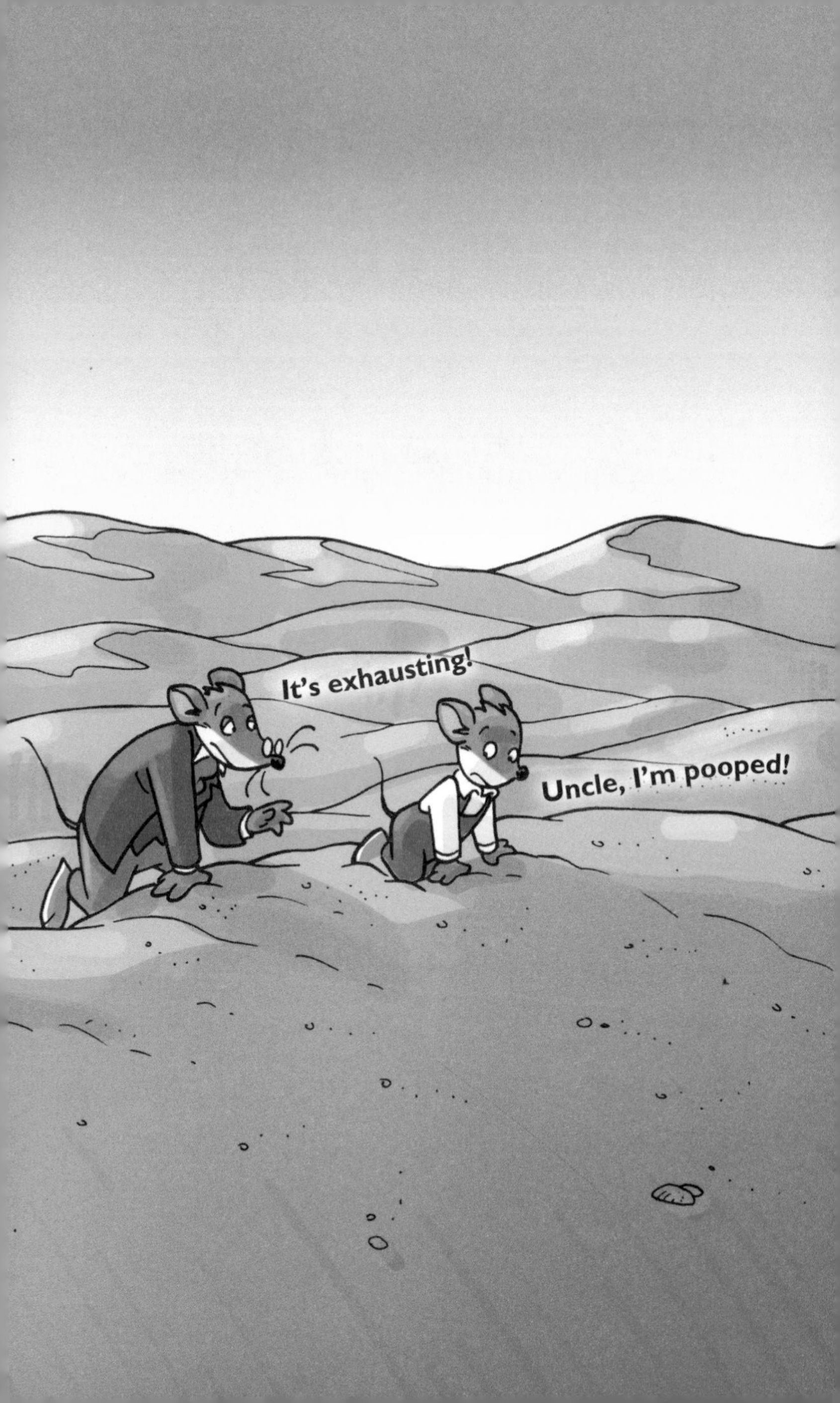
It's exhausting!
Uncle, I'm pooped!

A Terrible Sandstorm

We began trudging along in the HOT desert sand.

It was exhausting. My paws felt like two-ton blocks of cheddar. Rats! Just thinking about cheddar made my tummy GRUMBLE. I was tired and hungry and very, very thirsty. What I wouldn't have given for an ice-cold mozzarella milk shake!

"Can it get any WORSE?" I complained to no one in particular.

Trap scratched his head. "Well, actually, it could. I mean, we could be attacked by mouse-hungry aliens, bitten by a pack of stinging scorpions, or hit with a wild sandstorm," he suggested.

Just as Trap finished his sentence, the wind began to stir. Then swirl. Then howl. The sand **WHIPPED AROUND US**, making it impossible to move. Or see. Or breathe.

"SANDSTORM!" Thea shrieked. "Everyone stay close!"

Quickly, we huddled together. It was one giant group hug. The sand pelted us from every direction. We tied handkerchiefs around our snouts to keep from choking. Have you ever eaten a sand sandwich? Well, let me tell you, they are disgusting.

Everyone was coughing and gagging. I felt awful. It was all my fault we were caught in this terrible storm. Oh, why had I listened to that rotten rodent? My aunt Wary Whiskers always told me I was too trusting.

Just when it seemed like we were about to become permanent sand statues, I spotted two shadows approaching.

"Tuslaarai?" a voice called out.

Luckily, I knew a little Mongolian from reading that *Guide to Mongolia* on the plane. The word *tuslaarai* means "help."

I nodded my head.

I squeaked.

"Tuslaarai! Tuslaarai! Tuslaarai!"

MYSTERIOUS STRANGERS

We followed the two mysterious strangers. They led us to a large **tent**. It seemed to have sprung right out of the sand! How

amazing. Then I saw something even more AMAZING. The two strangers were young mouselets. They were the same age as my dear nephew Benjamin.

The mouselets brought us a canteen filled with fresh WATER. I was dying of thirst. But since I'm a gentlemouse, I let my

family drink first. My cousin, on the other paw, drank like a hog. He let out a loud burp when he was done. Can you believe we're related?

The mouselets introduced themselves. The boy was called Wanana and the girl was called Makido.

Wanana   Makido

Just then, two older rodents arrived. They were the young mouselets' parents, Tagik and Helela. We shook paws. It was so exciting to see how a real Mongolian family lived.

Helela explained that we were in a typical Mongolian **tent** known as a *gher*. The inside was painted **ORANGE**. Mongolians

Tagik

Helela

believe this color brings warmth and good luck. In the center of the tent was a WOODBURNING stove. It was used to cook and keep the mice warm. Helela told us that Mongols gather around the stove the same way we gather in front of the TV, but instead of watching, *they talk*. There were also several small **TABLES** used to serve tea on, many *paw-woven* rugs, and a **chest** for the lady of the house to keep her stuff in.

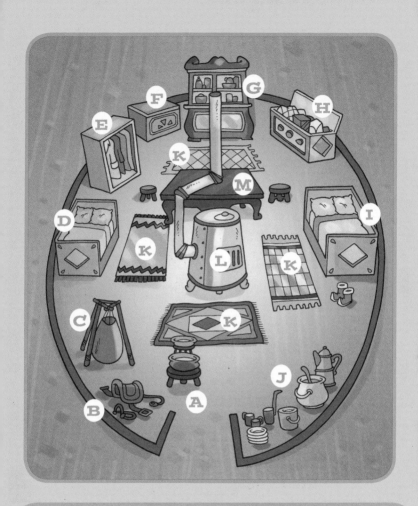

A. WATER BASIN

B. SADDLE AND HORSE GEAR

C. LEATHER CASKET TO FERMENT DONKEY'S MILK

D. CHILDRENS' BED

E. CLOSET FOR GUESTS

F. CHEST FOR THE HUSBAND'S THINGS

G. ARMOIRE FOR VALUABLE OBJECTS

H. CHEST FOR THE WIFE'S THINGS

I. PARENTS' BED

J. COOKWARE

K. RUGS

L. WOODBURNING STOVE

M. TABLE TO SERVE FOOD AND TEA ON

WARM MILK AND SALTY TEA

 Our new friends cooked us a delicious Mongolian dinner.

There were yummy SAUSAGES. Then we ate something called *buz*, which is like steamed meat-and-onion ravioli, and a salad made of **CABBAGE**. We drank warm mare milk and a salty tea.

The food was simple, but it hit the spot. And the Mongolians were **so kind and thoughtful**. We felt right at home!

"**YUMMY!**" "**BON APPÉTIT!**" "It looks delicious!" "Hooray!"

Trap felt so at home, he licked his plate

clean. How embarrassing! Luckily, the Mongolians took it as a compliment.

After supper, Helela told us a beautiful Mongolian legend. We all sat around the stove listening to the story. Meanwhile,

Benjamin played quietly with **Makido** and **Wanana**. Then he painted a picture using a stick dipped in **whortleberry** juice.

The Two Horses

There were two horses in the prairie heading toward greener pastures. One day, the older horse said, "I'm stopping here. You go on ahead by yourself, my young friend, and remember: Don't ever open any packages or sacks if you don't know exactly what's in them."

After he said this, they bid each other farewell. The young horse left at a gallop. Soon after, he found a great big sack in the middle of the road, and in spite of his old friend's warning, the young horse decided to open it.

What a mistake! A hungry, mean wolf jumped out of the sack, ready to devour him. Luckily, a much wiser rabbit happened to pass by, and he said to the wolf, "Excuse me, Mr. Wolf, were you really hidden inside that sack? I can't believe it! A strapping, muscular wolf like you couldn't fit in a sack so small!"

"Of course I can," said the wolf. "Do you want me to show you? Look!"

Having said this, he slipped inside the sack again.

Quickly, the rabbit tied the strings of the sack and the wolf found himself trapped again. From then on, the horse and the rabbit became great friends. If you are ever in a prairie, look closely, and maybe you'll see them running happily side by side!

IN THE VALLEY OF THE GIANT SKELETONS

When Helela finished her story, everyone clapped. Everyone except Trap, who was too busy **SLURPING** up more of the salty tea. Did I mention that my cousin can be totally embarrassing?

Then I asked our new friends if they could take us to the **Valley of the Giant Skeletons**.

Unfortunately, they **SHOOK** their heads. They didn't know where it was.

I chewed my whiskers sadly. Oh, why had I given Bondi Bobirat that map? Now we would never be able to find Uncle Wally's **TREASURE**.

Just then, a little paw tugged my sleeve. "Uncle Geronimo, I have a *surprise* for you," my nephew squeaked.

"I tried to *draw* it from memory," Benjamin explained. "It's the way to the Valley of the Giant Skeletons."

I clapped my paws. "THIS IS IT!" I cried. I gave my nephew a giant hug.

When Helela and Tagik saw the map, they nodded. "Yes, we can take you there." They both grinned.

It was very late, so it was decided that we

would leave at **DAWN**. We slept like, well, mice. The next day, we loaded the camels with **BLANKETS**, food, and canteens filled with water.

Let me tell you, I was not thrilled to get back on a camel. My tail kept getting **pinched** between the camel's humps. And every time we moved, I felt a little **motion sick**. Still, I couldn't help but notice the beautiful view. The sky was so **BLUE** and the sandy dunes seemed to sparkle.

Then I noticed something else shining besides just the sand. Was it really? Could it be?

Yes, it was the bones of a

... **GIANT SKELETON!**

UNCLE WALLY'S TREASURE!

I climbed down off the camel and brushed my paw over the giant **skeleton**. Holey cheese! It was incredible! For a moment, I was squeakless. I wondered what animal the skeleton belonged to.

When I found my voice, I called my friend Petunia Pretty Paws.

"What a find, Geronimo!" she cried. "That skeleton sounds like it could belong to a Tarbosaurus, a dinosaur similar to a *Tyrannosaurus rex*! What an extraordinary TREASURE!"

I was so thrilled, my fur was standing

on end. I, Geronimo Stilton, had made a MONUMENTAL scientific discovery! I couldn't wait to bring the bones back to New Mouse City. I couldn't wait to tell all of my friends at home. I couldn't wait to take a nice cold shower. Did I mention it was HOT and dusty in the desert?

Under the blazing sun, my family and I worked together, digging up the giant bones. It was hard work, but we were all excited. Well, everyone except for my cousin Trap. He's not big on scientific discoveries. Unless they involve GOLD, diamonds, or cold hard cash, that is.

Dinosaurs made their appearance about 230 million years ago during the Triassic period.

The first dinosaurs were small carnivores, only about as tall as German shepherds. They were able to stand erect and run very fast. Thanks to this characteristic, they were able to prevail over the reptiles that populated the earth before them. It was later on that the much larger herbivores first appeared.

At the start of the Jurassic period, about 200 million years ago, dinosaurs grew in size, number, and variety. At that time, the following appeared on Earth: *Shunosaurus*, gigantic herbivores with extremely long necks and tails like the *Diplodocus* and the *Brachiosaurus*; *Stegosaurus*, a herbivore armed with bony plates along the top of its back and spikes extending along its very long tail, much like the various types and sizes of carnivores, such as the *Allosaurus*; and flying reptiles like the *Pterodactyls* that

DIPLODOCUS

BRACHIOSAURUS

have large wings made of a membrane similar to those of modern-day bats.

At the end of the Late Cretaceous period, around 68 million years ago, one of the fiercest predators of all time appeared: *Tyrannosaurus rex.*

After having dominated the earth for 160 million years, the dinosaurs suddenly disappeared. Why? There are several hypotheses to explain their disappearance:

- The Earth was hit by a meteorite.

- There was a huge change in the climate, perhaps caused by a volcanic eruption.

- At the beginning of the Cretaceous period there were mammals that fed on dinosaur eggs.

The only certainty is that at the end of the Cretaceous period, the only species to survive were small birds, amphibians, marine animals, and small mammals.

TYRANNOSAURUS

STEGOSAURUS

DINOSAURS OF

About 130 million years ago, the Gobi Desert was a region with great lakes and rivers, and was richly populated by plants, animals, and various kinds of trees. Today, many of these fossils can be found in what is now a desert area. Fossilized dinosaurs and fish skeletons, turtles, and reptile eggs, have all been found. A fossil of a *Velociraptor*, a carnivorous predator, still holding its prey, a *Protoceratops*, in its claws, was found in Togrogun Shiree. Most likely, both died during the fight, and centuries later their bodies were found preserved together.

All the finds in this area have been very important to increasing our understanding of these extraordinary animals.

TARBOSAURUS SKELETON

One of the best-known dinosaurs is the *Tarbosaurus*. Because of their similarities, the Tarbosaurus could be considered a cousin to the *Tyrannosaurus rex*.

This two-footed carnivore, whose front feet are much smaller than its back feet, measured 30–36 feet in length and lived in the Gobi Desert. An extremely rare full skeleton has been found, as well as fossils with well-preserved skin!

ALONE IN THE GOBI DESERT

We worked all **DAY** and all **NIGHT**. At dawn, we put the bones in a **WOODEN** box and closed it with a lock. Now we had to figure out how we were going to get the box back home. I agreed to stay and guard it. Everyone else went looking for help.

I waved good-bye to my family. Then they disappeared over the **SAND DUNES**. I never felt so **ALONE** in my life! Days went by.

To make the time go faster, I . . .

1. reread the *Guide to Mongolia* 320 times.

2. told myself a ton of bad jokes.

3. sang "Squeak Goes the Hamster!" until I lost my voice.

4. practiced tying my tail in a sailor's knot.

5. counted the grains of sand under my paws.

None of these tricks worked very well. By the third day, I was so bored I thought I would go crazy. Oh, how I hate being alone!

I can't take being alone anymore!

WHAT DID THE TARBOSAURUS EAT?

Right then, as the sun was setting, I saw a dark shadow. It was headed straight for me.

Was it a ferocious, RODENT-EATING DESERT MONSTER? Was it an ALIEN SPACESHIP? Was this how it would all end? Headlines flashed before my eyes: STILTON STOLEN BY ALIEN BEINGS! PUBLISHER PERISHES IN THE PAWS OF A DEADLY DESERT CREATURE!

My stomach dropped. My whiskers twitched in terror. I closed my eyes. But when I opened them, I saw the most wonderful sight.

A grinning Dr. von Fossilsnout stood in front of me.

"Congratulations, *Mr. Stilton*! I just

got word that you have found a *precious* *Tarbosaurus* skeleton. Give me the key to that box, and I'll take over from here. I'm headed back to the **MOUSEUM OF NATURAL HISTORY** right now," she said.

Before I could reply, my cell phone *rang*. It was my friend *Petunia Pretty Paws*.

"Hello, G? Is that you? I have some **DISTURBING** news. I just spoke with the

mice at the Mouseum of Natural History. **Dr. von Fossilsnout** is not traveling. The rodent you met is a fake!" she squeaked.

I **gasped**. I stared at Dr. von Fossilsnout. Had she really been pulling my paw? Was she actually an imposter?

Petunia told me to ask the rodent a simple question about the **Tarbosaurus**. "If she's really an expert on dinosaurs, she'll know the answer," Petunia insisted.

I felt like a fool, but I knew Petunia was right. I had to find out the truth. Maybe it was all just one big misunderstanding.

Ask a simple question...

Ask her one question . . .

"Ahem, excuse me, Dr. von Fossilsnout," I began. "I hate to bother you. But would you mind telling me what the Tarbosaurus ate?" I said.

The doctor **STARED** at me with piercing **BLUE EYES**. Suddenly, she looked so familiar to me. If only I could put my paw on it.

"I don't have time for this, Mr. Stilton," she hissed. "Just give me the **KEY**. Now!"

Suddenly, I was filled with anger. Who did this rodent think she was? How dare she order me around!

I opened my mouth to protest, but nothing came out. Was I coming down with a cold? Had the cat got my tongue? No, I had just been **whacked** over the

What did the Tarbosaurus eat?

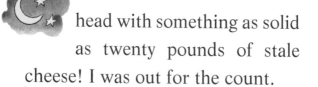

 head with something as solid as twenty pounds of stale cheese! I was out for the count.

A PRETTY GOOD KNOCK ON THE HEAD

When I came to, I was tied up like a furry hot dog.

Bondi Bobirat came out from behind the truck. He was holding an **ENORMOUS BONE**.

"Pretty good knock on the head, eh?" he said to the fake Dr. von Fossilsnout.

Pretty good knock on the head?

Now I was really **ENRAGED** and humiliated. Oh, why hadn't I listened to my family? They tried to tell me **BOBIRAT** was up to no good.

The fake **Dr. von Fossilsnout** smirked. "That's right, Stilton. Bondi Bobirat works for me. I knew you would lead us right to the **Tarbosaurus's** skeleton," she explained.

By now, my head was **spinning**. And it wasn't just from being **CLOBBERED**. I couldn't take my eyes off Dr. von Fossilsnout. Or whatever her name was. Those piercing blue eyes. The blonde fur. I just knew I had met her before.

The good, or should I say, bad doctor stared back at me, too. "Haven't you recognized me yet, Stilton?" she chuckled. Then she took off her tinted glasses and unpinned her blonde hair. She took off her khaki jacket. Underneath she wore a tight **BLACK JUMPSUIT**.

I almost fainted . . . again! What a **FOOL**

THE SHADOW

The Shadow is Sally Ratmousen's cousin. The Shadow is a fascinating rodent, but she will do anything to get rich. She's an expert in the art of disguise, and knows all the tricks to pass unnoticed. Geronimo met her in the adventures of The Mysterious Cheese Thief and The Mummy Without a Name.

I'd been. I would have recognized that rodent anywhere. It was the Shadow!

"I know you! You're the **SHADOW**!" I shouted.

Do you know the **THE SHADOW**?

She is one clever and famouse **thief**. I met her years ago on one of my many adventures.

She smiled with satisfaction. "Thanks for leading me to this **TREASURE**, Stilton," she squeaked. "Now all I have to do is sell this skeleton to a collector and I'll be rich, rich, rich!" ♥ ♥ ♥

I rolled my eyes. The **SHADOW** was so predictable. All she ever cared about was money.

Now scientists would never learn about the Tarbosaurus.

"How can you be so selfish?" I squeaked. But my words were drowned out by a loud roaring sound. It was coming from the ground. First it trembled. Then it shook.

Holey cheese! It felt like we were in the middle of an earthquake. But are there really earthquakes in the desert?

THE GHOSTS OF MONGOLIA

Before I could whip out my trusty *Guide to Mongolia* to check things out, a cloud of DUST appeared in the distance. Someone was coming on horseback. Well, no, it wasn't just someone. It was actually a lot of someones.

First came Thea, **Trap**, and *Benjamin*. Then **Tagik**, **Helela**, **Wanana**, and **Makido**. Other Mongolian rodents followed behind them.

Geronimo... ...don't give up!

They were riding strange-looking horses. The horses were short and muscular with thick manes. I recognized them. They were the Przewalski's horses, also known as the *takhi*, or the "Ghosts of Mongolia."

The tribal chief got off his horse and pointed at **THE SHADOW**.

"Stop right there, young ratling!" he ordered. "We will not allow you to steal the **Giant Skeleton**! It is part of the history of our land. It is a true scientific treasure for all to enjoy."

We're coming!

Hang on, Cousin!

Uncle!

Here we are!

A FRAGMENT OF BLUE AMBER

THE SHADOW and **BONDI BOBIRAT** were taken away. I know it's crazy, but part of me was sad to see the Shadow go. She's really not such a bad mouse, you know. I mean, she's **SMART**. She's *funny*.

In the name of our friendship.

Um, thanks.

She's *beautiful*. Now if she could just stop that bad habit she has of stealing things....

I was still thinking about the Shadow when the Mongolian tribal chief approached me. He gave me and every member of my family a gift. "Let these stone **pendants** symbolize our newfound friendship," he announced.

As soon as the chief left, my cousin began to grumble. "I can't believe I came all the way out here and didn't get **rich**. Now all I've got to show for my hard work is this silly old **rock**," he **complained**.

He was about to throw it away, when my sister grabbed his paw. "**Are your whiskers twisted**?" she shrieked. "This isn't just a rock. It's worth a fortune! Look closely: It's a fragment of **BLUE** amber. That's one precious stone. And inside is a fossilized insect!"

As soon as he realized the rock was valuable, Trap jumped up and did a little dance. "I'm rich! I'm rich!" he squeaked.

I rolled my eyes. Some things never change.

Then I stared at my own blue pendant. It shimmered and sparkled in my paw. It really was a beautiful symbol of FRIENDSHIP.

Amber is an organic material formed by the sap of prehistoric conifer trees. Plants and insects that were trapped in it are often perfectly preserved. Because of that, amber was considered a powerful and magical stone in the old days. It was thought that it held the beginning of life! The color varies from yellow to light brown with hues of blue, purple, and green. Blue amber is very rare.

Friendship Is a

Real friends... are rare... that's why... they're so.

True Treasure!

precious!...And when... you have them... you should never... let them go!

THE REAL DR. VON FOSSILSNOUT!

As soon as we returned to New Mouse City, we went directly to the **MOUSEUM OF NATURAL HISTORY**. The real Dr. von Fossilsnout met us in her office.

"Good morning, Mr. Stilton. Good morning, Stilton family. I am so HAPPY to meet all of you," she squeaked. We shook paws all around.

Then I presented Dr. von Fossilsnout with the giant *Tarbosaurus* **skeleton**. "I hope this will help you learn more about the history of dinosaurs," I said.

Dr. von Fossilsnout looked like she had just won the MOUSE LOTTERY.

She told us the dinosaur bones we had found were worth a fortune. "They are a true treasure," she marveled. "Thank you for donating this AMAZING discovery!"

She explained how the mouseum would mount the bones on **BRACKETS**. Then they would put them all together to look just like a real *Tarbosaurus*. She also said that they would make a PLAQUE to hang in front of the exhibit. It would say that the skeleton was donated by the Stilton Family. "And, of course, it will list all of your names," the doctor added.

"That's so cool! Wait until I tell all of my friends!" Benjamin cried, clapping his paws excitedly. We all laughed. Well, everyone except my cousin Trap. He had slipped off to the mouseum cafeteria and was busy stuffing his snout with cheese-filled doughnuts.

Before we left the mouseum, Benjamin

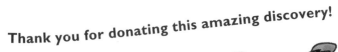

Thank you for donating this amazing discovery!

tugged at my paw.

"You know, I've been thinking, Uncle. Even though I would love to have my name on that plaque, the skeleton was really **UNCLE WALLY'S** discovery. We should only put his name on that sign," he said.

I was so **PROUD**. I gave Benjamin a giant hug.

DID I MENTION I HAVE THE...

SWEETEST LITTLE

NEPHEW ON ALL OF

MOUSE ISLAND?

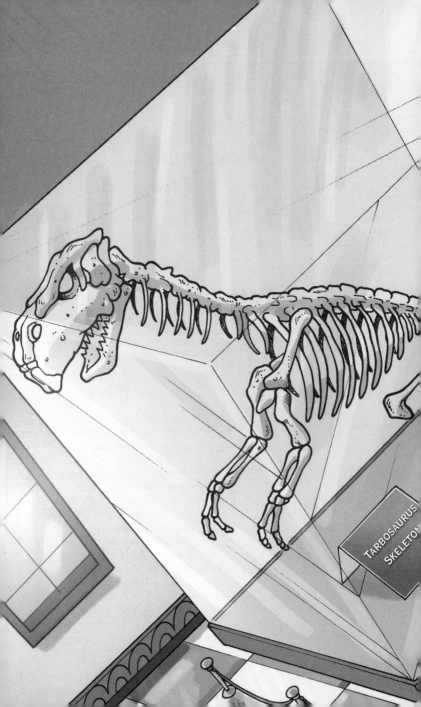

A Special Ceremony

A month later, we were invited to a special ceremony. The mouseum had completely assembled the bones we had found into a *Tarbosaurus* skeleton. A whole room was dedicated to this important scientific find.

THIS ROOM IS
DEDICATED TO THE MEMORY
OF WANDERING WALLY STILTON,
WHO DISCOVERED THE SECRET
OF THE VALLEY OF THE
GIANT SKELETONS.

The mayor of New Mouse City cut a *red ribbon* leading to the exhibit. I felt so proud to be part of such an important occasion!

I would never forget our **ADVENTURE** in Mongolia. And now the world would never forget

OUR INCREDIBLE UNCLE WALLY.

Want to read my next adventure?
It's sure to be a fur-raising experience!

GERONIMO AND THE GOLD MEDAL MYSTERY

I, Geronimo Stilton, am not a sportsmouse. Running? Sweating? Not for me. I prefer relaxing in an armchair with a bowl of cheesy chews and a good book. But when I was assigned to report on the Olympics in Greece, I sniffed a mysterious adventure in the making! And holey cheese, was I right....

And don't miss any of my other fabumouse adventures!

#1 Lost Treasure of the Emerald Eye

#2 The Curse of the Cheese Pyramid

#3 Cat and Mouse in a Haunted House

#4 I'm Too Fond of My Fur!

#5 Four Mice Deep in the Jungle

#6 Paws Off, Cheddarface!

#7 Red Pizzas for a Blue Count

#8 Attack of the Bandit Cats

#9 A Fabumouse Vacation for Geronimo

#10 All Because of a Cup of Coffee

#11 It's Halloween, You 'Fraidy Mouse!

#12 Merry Christmas, Geronimo!

#13 The Phantom of the Subway

#14 The Temple of the Ruby of Fire

#15 The Mona Mousa Code

#16 A Cheese-Colored Cam

#17 Watch Your Whiskers, Stilton!

#18 Shipwreck on the Pirate Islands

#19 My Name Is Stilton, Geronimo Stilton

#20 Surf's U Geronimo

#21 The Wild, Wild West

#22 The Secret of Cacklefur Castle

A Christmas Tale

#23 Valentir Day Disast

Field Trip to
agara Falls

#25 The Search for
Sunken Treasure

#26 The Mummy
with No Name

#27 The Christmas
Toy Factory

8 Wedding
Crasher

#29 Down and Out
Down Under

#30 The Mouse
Island Marathon

#31 The Mysteriou
Cheese Thief

Christmas
atastrophe

*and
coming
soon*

#33 Geronimo
and the Gold
Medal Mystery

ABOUT THE AUTHOR

Born in New Mouse City, Mouse Island, Geronimo Stilton is Rattus Emeritus of Mousomorphic Literature and of Neo-Ratonic Comparative Philosophy. For the past twenty years, he has been running *The Rodent's Gazette*, New Mouse City's most widely read daily newspaper.

Stilton was awarded the Ratitzer Prize for his scoops on *The Curse of the Cheese Pyramid* and *The Search for Sunken Treasure*. He has also received the Andersen 2000 Prize for Personality of the Year. One of his bestsellers won the 2002 eBook Award for world's best ratlings' electronic book. His works have been published all over the globe.

In his spare time, Mr. Stilton collects antique cheese rinds and plays golf. But what he most enjoys is telling stories to his nephew Benjamin.

THE RODENT'S GAZETTE

1. Main entrance

2. Printing presses (where the books and newspaper are printed)

3. Accounts department

4. Editorial room (where the editors, illustrators, and designers work)

5. Geronimo Stilton's office

6. Storage space for Geronimo's books

Map of New Mouse City

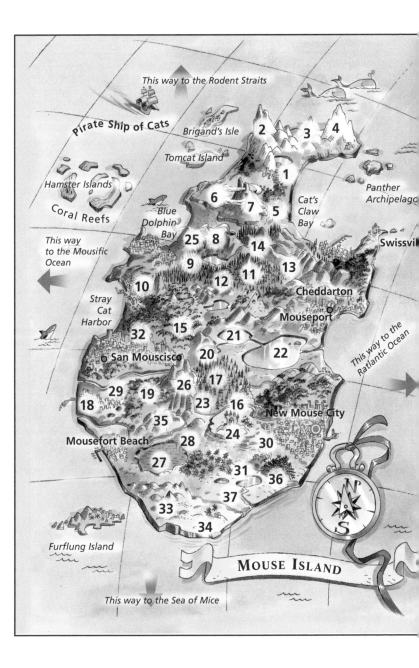

Map of Mouse Island

1. Big Ice Lake
2. Frozen Fur Peak
3. Slipperyslopes Glacier
4. Coldcreeps Peak
5. Ratzikistan
6. Transratania
7. Mount Vamp
8. Roastedrat Volcano
9. Brimstone Lake
10. Poopedcat Pass
11. Stinko Peak
12. Dark Forest
13. Vain Vampires Valley
14. Goose Bumps Gorge
15. The Shadow Line Pass
16. Penny Pincher Castle
17. Nature Reserve Park
18. Las Ratayas Marinas
19. Fossil Forest
20. Lake Lake
21. Lake Lakelake
22. Lake Lakelakelake
23. Cheddar Crag
24. Cannycat Castle
25. Valley of the Giant Sequoia
26. Cheddar Springs
27. Sulfurous Swamp
28. Old Reliable Geyser
29. Vole Vale
30. Ravingrat Ravine
31. Gnat Marshes
32. Munster Highlands
33. Mousehara Desert
34. Oasis of the Sweaty Camel
35. Cabbagehead Hill
36. Rattytrap Jungle
37. Rio Mosquito

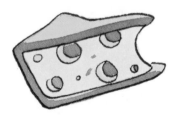

Dear mouse friends,
Thanks for reading, and farewell
till the next book.
It'll be another whisker-licking-good
adventure, and that's a promise!

Geronimo Stilton